EVOLVE
THE BEGINNING OF CHANGE

RAGHAVI JHANJEE

BLUEROSE PUBLISHERS
India | U.K.

Copyright © Raghavi Jhanjee 2024

All rights reserved by author. No part of this publication may be reproduced, stored in a retrieval system or transmitted in any form or by any means, electronic, mechanical, photocopying, recording or otherwise, without the prior permission of the author. Although every precaution has been taken to verify the accuracy of the information contained herein, the publisher assume no responsibility for any errors or omissions. No liability is assumed for damages that may result from the use of information contained within.

BlueRose Publishers takes no responsibility for any damages, losses, or liabilities that may arise from the use or misuse of the information, products, or services provided in this publication.

For permissions requests or inquiries regarding this publication, please contact:

BLUEROSE PUBLISHERS
www.BlueRoseONE.com
info@bluerosepublishers.com
+91 8882 898 898
+4407342408967

ISBN: 978-93-6783-118-2

Cover design: Daksh
Typesetting: Tanya Raj Upadhyay

First Edition: December 2024

Dedicated to my family and friends

Author: *Raghavi Jhanjee*
Illustrated by: *Anusree Ghosh*
Art Direction: *Abhirup Chowdhury*

ABOUT THE BOOK

Embark on a poetic odyssey with "Evolve," the second gem in the Embrace series.

This book is about changes and growing from those changes.

When life throws curveballs at you and you still manage to stay afloat, you evolve.

Explore a journey of self-discovery and acceptance, where each verse is a brushstroke on the canvas of life's twists and turns.

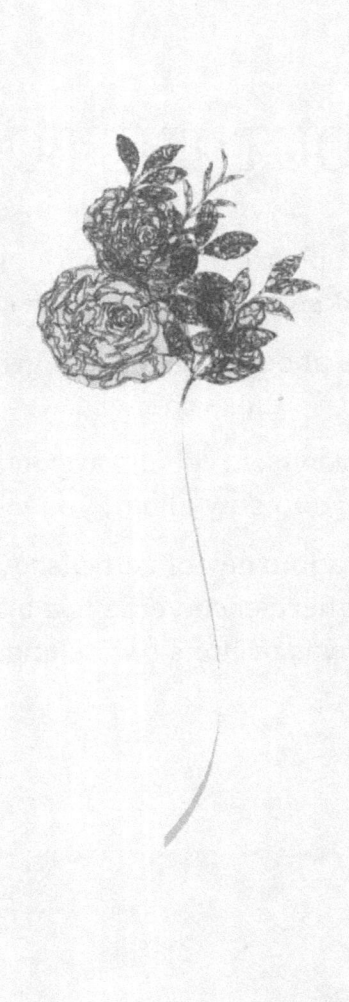

Table of Contents

THE PURSUIT 1
CONNECTIONS 57

THE PURSUIT

Change is unending, and so is its pursuit.

CHANGES

Change is scary.
Change is sudden.
Change is gradual.
Change is evident.
Change can leave you in tears
In laughter,
In confusion,
In uncertainty.
You love some changes,
You dislike some.
You want some to reverse,
You want some to stay.
Change is tricky,
Change is true,
Change is overwhelming,
Change is cruel.
A person can have 100 shades to him,
And you've only deciphered a few.
Make note of changes,
Make note of what's positive and what's not.
Some things you let go,
Some things you don't.
Some things you allow to get sour,
Some things you sweeten every day.
Changes.
They can leave you high and dry.
They can leave you whole
Changes don't take your permission.
They occur.

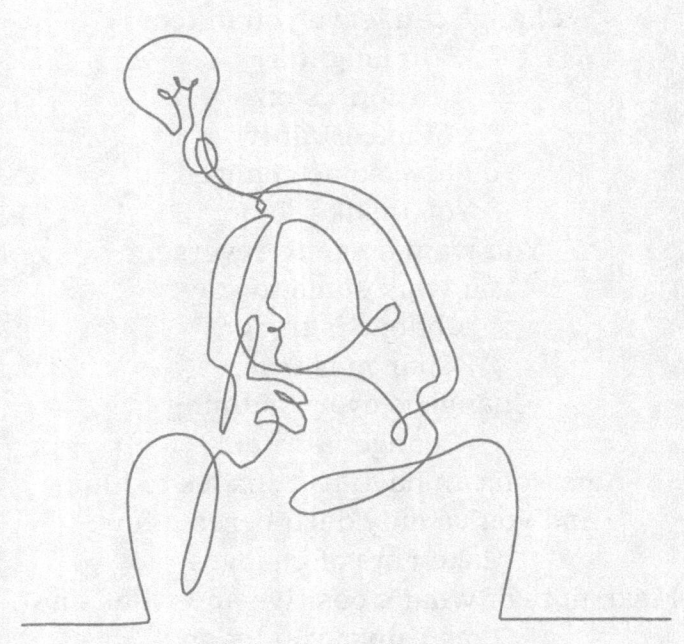

IDEA

Longing for an idea,
I search surfaces, spaces and depths of content.
Hoping that something strikes a chord with me,
It sparks a fire that turns into something big.
With every sliver fully explored,
Broken down into nuances and situations,
Creativity oozing out through and through.
Longing for an idea,
I finally start to scribble down,
Till I get what I was looking for.

WORKING OUT

They say I am not visible,
Even when I see my words up there.
They say nothing is yours,
Even though my pen weeps for
acknowledgement.
They often check up on me,
To see if I am doing anything at all.
They say a lot of things,
But in a world of politics,
Hard-work suffocates.
Effort pressed under layers and jealousy,
No room for growth.
How do I fight?
If you put me behind the bars,
Without letting me claim my craft.
They say I am not visible.
How will I be?
Do you let me be?
A mere writer has only words to give,
But those are his words and his alone,
Struggling to be claimed in this world of politics.

WHO AM I?

Who am I?
What am I?
What do they think about me?
Does it really matter?
A sliver of a silver lining always fades away,
Just when I try to grab it.
Can't think no more,
When it's a dead end I always meet.
I've given my all,
Yet I am scorned, doubted and blamed.
My mind has stopped to function,
My heart is stopping to feel.
I am scared to change into a person I am not,
Because of people who put me through pain.
I open my book every time,
Only to get hurt,
Only to feel like a nobody,
Only to feel pain.
It's all a blur,
As my parched throat refuses to speak,
As my eyes can't see clear,
As my mind can't think any more,
Incomplete feels complete now.

9 TO 9

It's like you are working towards a dead end,
When you slog and you win alone ....
They see you struggle on your own,
A one woman army,
Who goes unnoticed day in and day out.
Looking for a ray of appreciation for giving her all,
Looking for the slightest amount of acknowledgement for putting in those extra nights all alone.
Others they have a team,
While she dusts and shines alone.
Her world is a small one but too daunting to take in,
Where people know she works alone,
But choose to ignore telling her worth,
To let her know once in a while that she is doing her best,
And it's much appreciated.
It's like she is working towards a dead end,
Slogging, teary-eyed, hoping to see the sunrise as she spends it all inside stuck to a screen typing away her life.

DEEP INTO THE WORDLE

My words are raw,
They are tired of being refined.
They are tired of being filtered and screened.
Their beauty is now a thing of the past,
As they are out to be sold to ungrateful eyes,
To people who care to a minimal extent,
To people who skip what doesn't appeal to them.
My words have lost emotion,
You've suffocated them with deadlines,
A creative sucked out of creativity has no value.
It isn't roses and daisies,
It's a field of sunflowers with invisible
thorns that prick you blindly.

HEAL

I fear this streak of self-destruction,
That slowly crawls up my skin.
This streak is a wildfire,
Causing all the good things to come to an end,
And showing the way out to all the good people in my life.
I fear to not have the strength to fight this poison inside of me,
It leaves me in guilt,
And yet I do not know what triggers it.
I have thought time and again about what I truly want,
But I am left with unclear answers.
I am bruised inside out,
And I don't know how to heal.
So I self-destruct the only good things,
That help me to be me, to be sane,
to feel good.
Self-love has become something unfamiliar to me now,
As I try to escape from something,
And then fall again head-first.
I want my bruises to breathe,
So they finally start to heal.
I don't want to be the bad guy anymore.

16

THE WINDOW

I have been looking out the window,
The window has stories to tell,
People to reveal,
While I navigate how I feel.
Can things ever be so simple?
I question now and then,
Can poems feel complete?
When you write them with half a heart...
For unresolved thoughts shout in your head,
As you look out the window,
Staying still while the world keeps moving outside.

UNFILTERED

If I could write my unfiltered story,
I would write about all the ups and downs.
The clowns, the shrewd, the egoistic buffalos, the ungrateful, the bossy, the sexist pigs,
the masked abusers, the anxiety givers,
the sarcastic know-it-all's, low-life's and so much more.
If I could write my unfiltered story,
I would write about my downfall, struggle, fearlessness, courage, fear, anger, sadness, love, happiness
and other emotions felt at every pitstop.
It's strange how people can be something in front of your face,
And change on seeing authority.
How they can use you selfishly,
And then leave you blue.
Their devils come bearing smiles,
Their laughter hides evil intentions.
If I could write my unfiltered story,
I would write about how love salvaged me,
Of how I defeated evil,
Of how I found my strength when I felt alone,
Of how I stood up for what I believed,
Of how negativity couldn't pierce through me,
And of how I flew, touching the skies
Being limitless and free.

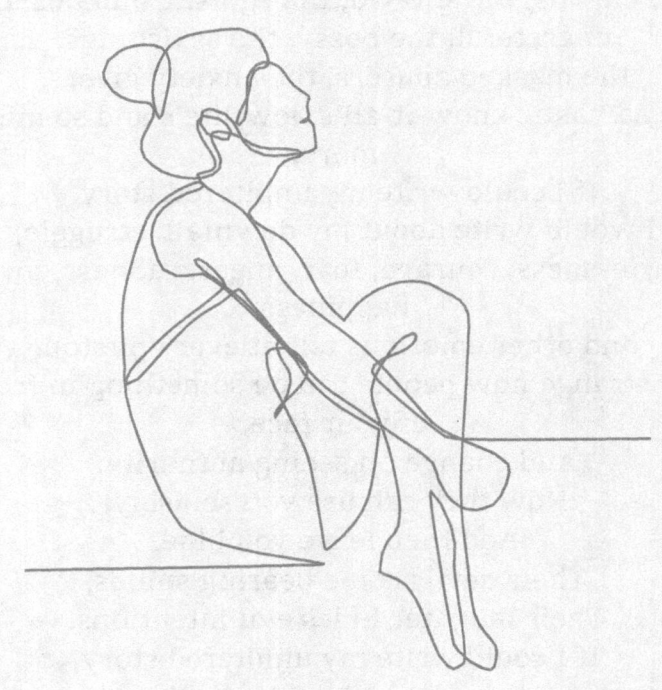

WAVE

Emptiness is what I feel,
When there is noise,
When there is silence.
I cave in to my surroundings,
But I detach internally.
Loving the warmth while it lasts,
But then longing for the cold.
For some embraces are momentarily comforting,
But fail to fall under long-term duration.
I have been quite reckless lately,
Rebelling against how cautious I've been.
The wrongs have felt right,
But have left me completely empty.
I don't know what I want anymore,
But I still keep going on.
I'm the wave that never rests by the bay.

FREE-FLOW, FREE-FLAW

Don't feel too deeply,
Don't hurt too intensely,
It's a little too much to take in already.
Let your gentle heart feel at ease,
Take deeper breaths to let it go.
Close your eyes for pauses,
For pauses are the roadway to clarity.
De-clutter the noise of people's opinions,
Cry in silence or cry out loud,
It's okay to.
Remember that.
Uncomplicate your life.
Smoothen the creases that you unknowingly created,
And flow with the carefree wind.
See where the calmness takes you,
And give in just this once.
Blank.
Blank.
Blank.
You're the sailor of your ship
So take it where you want.
The pace doesn't matter,
As long as you are content.

BACK TO THE HILLS

I've been longing those school days in the hills,
Where the winters exude warmth,
And friends were a close-knit family.
Where even though I wasn't searching,
I found myself.
The windy evenings reminded me,
Of those days when we were up to mischief.
Not a soul tattle-tale,
Carefree and focused.
Somehow ending up in trouble always.
I've been longing those school days in the hills,
Where life happened,
The memories never fade,
Of hustling, growing up, laughing, discovering
and so much more.
In those foggy skies,
Those midnight adventures after lights out,
Those intense basketball practice sessions,
Munching wai-wai during study-time,
And eagerly waiting for Sundays, projects,
picnics, dance parties and trekking trips.
I found the best version of myself.
Those memories are not only found in the
pictures,
But are forever etched in my heart.

THESE WORDS OF MINE

My words are home to both darkness and light,
My mind is home to running thoughts craving my attention.
It gets blurry sometimes when you stand alone at your doorstep,
Or stare across an empty room,
Not feigning attention, just some clarity.
The fan circles on its highest speed,
Numbing the natural rush of the wind.
My hands feel tied up although free,
My throat forms lumps preventing speech.
My words are home to both darkness and light,
They look for company and comfort,
With full stops they become complete.
My words silence the chaos in my mind,
And my heart learns to love then unlove.
It's funny how my only form of true expression,
Is sometimes the hardest to express.
Like the words in my mind get lost in ink,
Just like my life that takes sharp turns in a blink.

TICKING

The moonlight floods into the darkness in my room,
But my soul remains in two minds.
Fighting over which side overpowers the other,
I turn and change positions,
Struggling to close my eyes and shut my mind,
Because it loves working during the night,
Like a restless guard on his daily rounds.
Falling back on the past and cycling into the future,
Cluelessly dishing out on the present.
Those 'no regrets' surface as regrets in the night,
Those 'shrugged off' minor mistakes surface as the unforgettable pricking instruments.
So I choose to open my eyes till my eyelids feel heavy enough,
And my soul feels drowsy enough,
To let go and slip into the subconscious.
For an empty cup is a myth,
Tiny granules do stay back to keep your clock ticking.

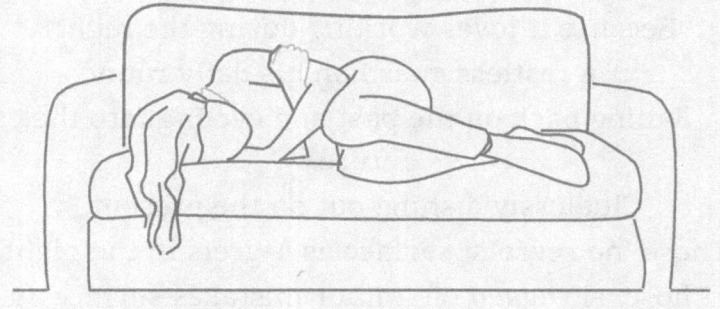

WEEKENDS

Just one of those days,
When I feel nothing.
A blank canvas
sitting without the bustle of colours.
A lazy afternoon,
Pausing the usual hustle.
Letting the music flirt with my ears,
As I extend my hand to grab some rays of the sun,
My cold hands embrace the warmth,
And regain their un-wrinkled natural self.
Sometimes you need to let go and lay back,
For plans change,
And unplanned things are more beautiful.
For they are far from the boundaries of your expectations,
They take you by surprise,
And sometimes just sometimes,
You need to let time flow.
Letting moments float,
As you breathe in each moment slowly.
Just like when I start to write,
Sometimes I don't know where to end a poem.
So I let words unfold and decide their destination.
On this cold Sunday morning,
I let myself free,
And do nothing for a change.

ROLL THE DICE

Roll me a dice,
Let's see what it brings this time.
Is it the everyday curveballs?
Or the last minute pressure cookers,
Or the one that fails expectations,
Or something just out of the blue.
Roll me a dice.
Will you now?
I have seen it all,
I can take it,
I can simply roll it back on,
Make it tumble on,
Let it toss on,
Without tossing myself.
The next time you bring a problem,
Roll me a dice first.
Will you?

LEARNING REALITY

It was time for distance to take matters in its own hands,
Clearly I wasn't learning.
Time did warn me subtly,
But I always thought this time it's different.
They rode on my tears,
And laughed as I shared my feelings.
For in their world being fake was second nature,
But not just to me.
Too many experiences do teach you a thing or two in the trade,
So you start to laugh when they laugh,
And hide those tears behind words.
You crack a joke or two,
Even though your heart is clearly not happy in their company anymore.
Trust is a thing so fictional in my book,
So I write till I stop feeling numb.
I stay wide awake till my eyelids shut under heaviness,
And at times I wish it wasn't so complicated.
So difficult.
To get people to be understanding, kind and most of all genuine.
I feel so much.
I lock it inside.
I keep it down.
No one walked beside me to listen.
The pain they have caused will only turn into my growth.
Onward and upward.
A new morning and I'll rise.

IN THE NIGHT

The moonlight floods into the darkness in my room,
But my soul remains in two minds.
Fighting over which side overpowers the other,
I turn and change positions,
Struggling to close my eyes and shut my mind,
Because it loves working during the night.
Like a restless guard on his daily rounds,
Falling back on the past and cycling into the future.
Cluelessly dishing out on the present,
Those 'no regrets' surface as regrets in the night,
Those shrugged off minor mistakes surface as the unforgettable pricking instruments.
So I choose to open my eyes till my eyelids feel heavy enough,
And my soul feels drowsy enough,
To let go and slip into the subconscious.
For an empty cup is a myth,
Tiny granules do stay back to keep your clock ticking.

THE DREAM I FEAR

I walk in my dreams,
Dreams concocted from everyday realities.
I see humans drastically change,
Shut behind closed doors,
Sitting inside stuffed rooms,
Consuming the virtual world one click at a time,
At peace with mundane routines.
I see a frail hand clutching on to pennies,
On roadsides that haven't seen a soul lately.
The sky now masked with a consistent fog,
Doesn't seem to float in eyes peeping from windows in transit.
Just yesterday was when the pyres stood piled up;
Of those who gasped for oxygen,
who fought and begged till life slipped out of their lungs.
In another part, crowds pile up;
To breathe in hilly winds,
The cries of survival seem forgotten
As ashes now merge with the soil.
Businesses in full throttle strive,
Not in humanity's stride;
While crowds turn a blind eye
To the future that warns to be more fatal
A little soldier stands up for life.

I struggle in my dream battling the drops on the edge of my eyes,
I continue walking into a soulless land,
That seems to be our near future.
As the Earth seems to breed an army of introverts,
Cocooned in their shells that scream comfort in isolation,
Where they prefer to type in words,
Instead, speak from mouths that have moved on from conversations.
Is the human touch now being replaced?
Getting lost behind screens that stay bright day and night,
Masking rooms with pretence backgrounds
Just as they mask how they feel.
This world scares me,
I call out for people to open their doors, their hearts, their mouths
But I fail, I fall.
I crawl to hold my phone as I battle the darkness closing in on me,
Not a soul efforts to cross their threshold,
As I crave the human light.
What are we turning into?

Businesses in full throttle strive,
Not in humanity's stride;
While crowds turn a blind eye
To the future that warns to be more fatal
A little soldier stands up for life.
I struggle in my dream battling the drops on the edge of my eyes,
I continue walking into a soulless land,
That seems to be our near future.
As the Earth seems to breed an army of introverts,
Cocooned in their shells that scream comfort in isolation,
Where they prefer to type in words,
Instead, speak from mouths that have moved on from
Will we ever cross the threshold?
Will this change stop while time fleets?
My fists stay clenched,
As my thoughts intensify.
I struggle to push away the darkness,
And grab the daylight.
I walk out of my dream,
Only to witness the change in humans that I fear.

GROWING

A seed was nurtured,
With a lot to learn from scars and survive storms.
From shutting of doors to pushing to open one,
Feeling dazed and confused,
Shattered but still unfazed by failure.
The other seedlings grew with him,
They made it a home away from home,
With endless laughter and silent sobs,
With pointless quarrels to staying up all night.
At times they lost their breath and their path but found comfort in each other,
Finding hard to grow up,
Mostly not sure about whether they were ready to grow up.
And in the most clueless moments, they found themselves.
A little grown-up than the day before,
A little hopeful than when they started,
They felt changes in everything.
It took courage, understanding and acceptance.
A storm appeared,
It changed the world they had planned.
Suddenly they felt stranded on a journey that felt like a never-ending stop,

Warmth vanished from the tips of their fingers as they held onto screens.
Screens that captured people but failed emotions,
The longing got real,
Their dreams became distant.
Uncertainty looming over them, no idea about the next step.
Will phones sustain bonds grown from love, care and sadness?
They steer clear of doubts as time heals,
They are holding onto faith,
They are holding onto hope,
They fear these changes,
They are growing into trees,
Trying each day, smiling through their tears.

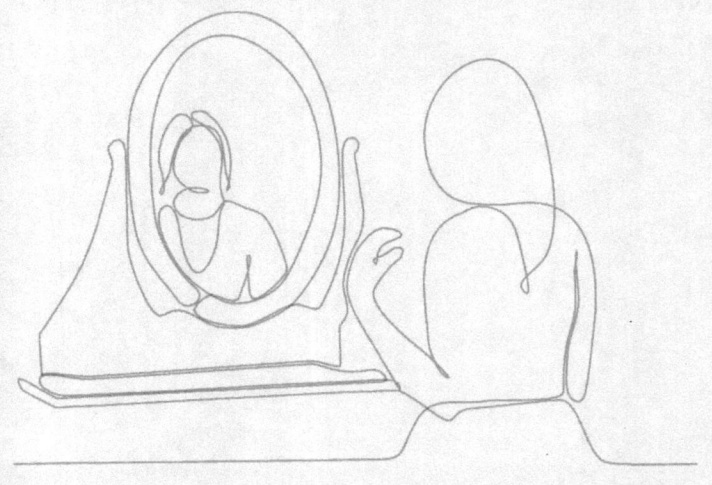

FOG

The fog on the mirror slowly descends,
And it becomes clearer.
The unanswered questions that lingered for long,
Seems to piece themselves with answers.
The constant whirlwind inside of me,
Turn silent to be at peace.
Those unsure whispers in my ears,
Have now found the strength to be heard.
Those pages that stood unsure of the words written in a rather stormy state,
Now proudly showcase them in fresh and crisp pages.
Confession does lead to conclusion,
If only you let the fog descend from your mirror.

DISTANT

I call myself a storyteller, a poet, a weaver of words.
But days on end I feel mute like words just don't cross my string of thought.
Like my mind sits empty wanting to write,
But nothing feels good enough.
Not a soul tells me their daily stories, not a soul shares their sorrows.
I think they all feel empty inside and now refuse to let
it show,
See that's the game that distance plays.
Where first you lose contact, then heart and slowly you feel comfortable in your contactless shell,
When a slightest bit of contact feels like a lot of effort
that you can't put in,
And so you habituate a life that is distant, closed up.
Why can't we share silence?
Why can't we share pain?
Why can't we share emptiness?
Is it so important to always have something to talk about?
Have we lost patience in just being there, for once?
People still crave to talk to each other,
But they are not ready to burst the bubble they have created.
The world is turning contactless and so are we..

A CHAOTIC WORKPLACE IS TOXIC TOO

The lines of instructions get lost
in strings of unorganised communication.
The work is duplicated and hence the effort.
Clarity of job role in the offer letter is present,
But it becomes unclear when you start working.
Mundane writing gets to your creative juices,
Making them sour, dull-coloured.
It is chaos with too many directions, too many tasks not streamlined,
Filling sheets with words that start to make no sense.
Jumping from one client to another,
Clouding my ongoing line of thought with
new ones flooding my work table,
It's a miss.
Yes I missed the point.
The job.
The unclear instruction.
But in chaos the ownership is one-sided,
Melodious vague instructions paired with blame-game,
At one instant you gain experience but in the very next you mess up.
Because the unorganised mess gets to you at some point.
So you end up messing up the messed.
For a chaotic workplace is toxic too.

PLAYING WITH WORDS

You play with fire,
Like I play with my words.
They dance on my tunes,
They adapt to my moods.
On some days they disappear,
They say they lay low to let my thoughts breathe.
My words are my strength,
My support on dreary days, friends on days of joy.
They speak my mind,
They freeflow,
They break but never let go.

CONNECTIONS

You can't do with them, you can't do without them.

IMPRINTS

In the night you said you love me,
In the day you effortlessly discarded me like your
used clothes tossed in your laundry bag.
Every day I ask if you are well,
You make love and then brew hate.
You tangle me, wrangle me and strangle me.
You bring me close only to throw me out with full force.
With you some days feel all rosy,
But the others remind me of my past.
Triggers, tremors, shivers I don't feel my heart beating.
I don't feel my lungs breathing,
Just feel strong hands engulf me whole.
Like I was a thing,
And they were human.
My thoughts haunt me,
As I try to let go of the marks still visible to me,
Every inch feels fresh as you make the wounds come alive.
Every time I shed a tear,
There is a chilling yet familiar current that passes through
my body's tips,
As if out of control.
In the night you again breathe down my neck,
And it feels okay at that moment.
But what is love I often wonder.
Is it what you speak?
Or
Is it the wounds that silently shout?
Today, tomorrow and whenever.

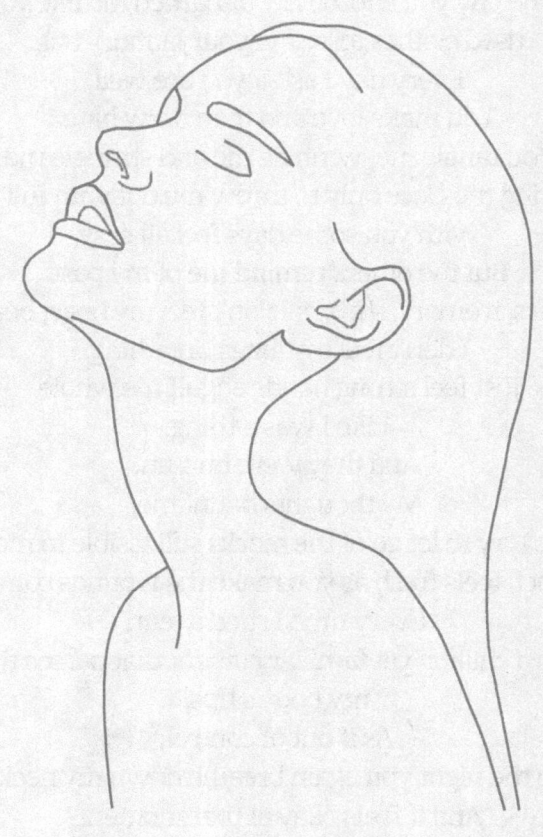

RUIN IS THE NEW HEAL

The pain is excruciating,
Invisible but just as real as anything else.
We're all broken figures walking towards the same old things,
We want the same old things,
Afraid to take the plunge,
Because we fear being shattered.
We've bandaged our broken,
We have managed to put up a brave face.
As we swipe, swipe, swipe,
Waiting to be ruined yet again.
It's moving fast inside out,
I navigate through the blur,
Not wanting to think yet ending up thinking.
We're all dead inside,
Zombies in an apocalypse.
So hold me close today as well,
As you leave the next day...

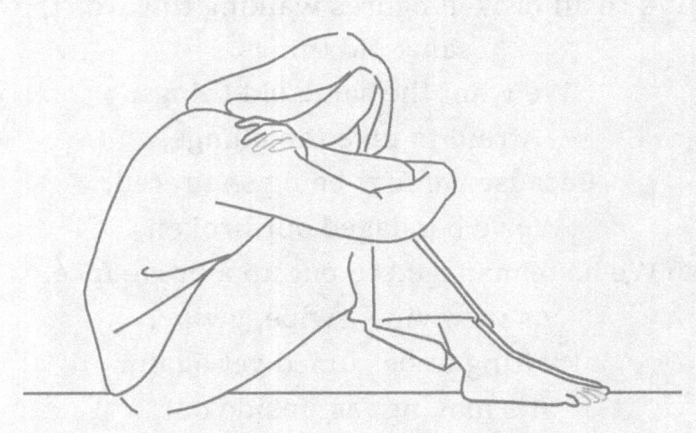

IN MY THOUGHTS

I tell him not,
That I think about him often.
We agreed it wouldn't be butterflies and roses,
I wonder though if there's a possibility of something more.
You refuse time and again,
But you don't realise we're silently drawn towards each other.
So just because of the fear of getting hurt,
Should I stop thinking about us?
Should I stop my feelings from feeling too much?
Should I put a stopper on the door?
So that you knock but can't enter no more.
I won't tell you ever,
What my little heart holds.
A secret I will hold on to for as long as
I can,
Because I fear losing what we have.
So I tell him not,
That I think about him often.

LIES

You're a liar,
You lie to everyone around you.
You push the blame on me.
But they see you now,
So no more hiding.
I see you now,
So no more protecting you.
You look for me still,
Even when you said you won't anymore.
You're a liar.
Thick skinned.
Double-faced.
Wannabe hero.
They see me raw and real,
So they can't handle it.
You hide under layers,
To be heroic.
Lately you've been shedding your skin,
But you've always been a snake, haven't you?
Don't play this game of peekaboo,
We're grown up now,
Might as well face the truth.
Apologies, you're still immature.
You've got truths that you're too scared to admit.
So let me be the devil that I am.
While you deceive with your angel eyes.

LOSING

I lost track of you first,
And then the train of my words.
As I slide my finger down my right arm,
Wanting to feel the same.
I shut my eyes but my heart hardly gives in.
I crave those shivers down my spine,
But they have long gone.
The dryness in your heart has absorbed my warmth.
Your sealed lips speak so much more than they ever have,
As your eyes wander in directions I'm not part of.
The strokes of my pen cluelessly hit the pages,
Its core, completely blank.
I lost track of you first,
And then the train of my words.

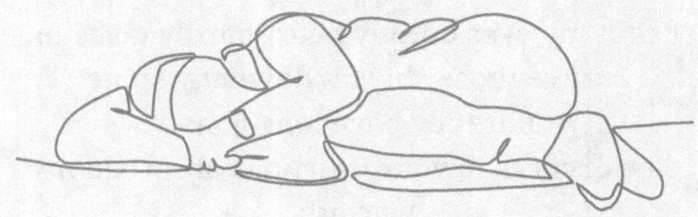

LAYING LOW

I lay low,
For on most days,
I am a silent wreck that refuses to shout her woes.
I lay low,
For they silence me if I speak too much,
I lay low.
For they've asked me to,
I lay low.
As walls cave in and hands reach out to shadow me,
I lay low.
As I try to stay afloat, necessary enough to keep breathing,
I lay low.
As they measure my clothes and my words,
I lay low.
For my privacy doesn't exist, all of it, they demand to know,
I lay low.
As I lose my memory of being free, of flying,
of colouring different colours, of launching endless dreams.
I lay low.
Ripped to shreds, forced to never oppose.

WORDING MY HEART OUT

Every day I play with words,
As if they understand me.
Like no one could.
They dance to my tunes.
Most times broken and abrupt,
Just like the sentences that form in my mouth,
But curl up into a smile,
Or sheer annoyance.
Words tingle my skin,
Sensations physically unknown.
I look closely as I write, then type,
Biting my lip, as I backspace words,
That pleaded to stay.
To stay with promises untold.
They tell tales of unforgiven heartbreaks,
They shout of silent suppressed angered woes,
They screech tyres that lured them into unfulfilling chatter,
Wound up in meanings they couldn't make sense of,
Wound up with people they hardly feel anything for.
As they hide away their true feelings,
To make things work,
As honest relationships turn into a thing of the past.
I play with my words,
Not sure what will last,
My words, they make sense to me,
Like no human ever could.

GROWING APART

The clock strikes 3. It's dark.
My mind-
Still meddled in the undertones of a dormant writing streak.
I've flipped through pages to shut out the world.
Lately, I flipped through thoughts shutting out the pages.
The faint light from my phone is no more frequent.
I wonder what's wrong.
I always thought distance could make one realise the value of warm hands and familiar shoulders.
We've grown distant instead.
Is this temporary?
Or a forever change of heart.
Crowds are suffocating, now.
Clinking glasses, faking laughter and empty chatter,
Living virtually midst reality.
Clutching to things I fail to relate to.
The music seems like noise and
I'm overwhelmed with the feeling of detachment.
Quietened down,
I hardly recognise myself.
Breathing motionless into colourless fleeting moments.
Finding silence in sound,
And sound in silence.

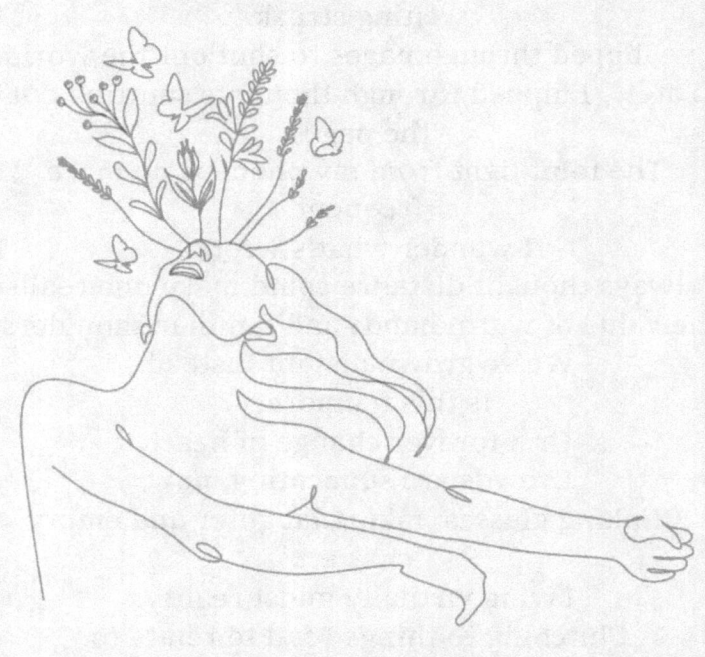

FOGGY MIND CONSTRUED TALES

I tiptoe in the blinding darkness,
Unsure of direction and destination.
I overthink a dozen half-baked thoughts,
Hoping to complete something in vain.
The dingy cells overpower flowery fields,
The mind is the master,
As it feeds on your subconscious.
Figuring out only to be tangled further,
They say do what your heart says,
But my heart fails to be loud enough.
A silent wreck,
As the mind masters its every move,
And I tiptoe into the blinding darkness,
Unsure of direction and destination.

I TOLD HER SO.

I told her so.
Time and again.
But her heart continued to ache,
For those who were heartless.
She would sit and wonder at the window sill,
And walk away disappointed.
The lock of her cage was tightening,
And again I told her to let go.
Expectations kill you slowly,
They laughed and rejoiced,
While she waited.
People come as they please, get attached and detached conveniently.
Act cold, act fake, act heartless.
But, she wouldn't understand,
That I had warned her before,
To choose her happiness instead of momentary happiness created through artificial beings.
I told her so.
That not all people were worth her care, love and so much more.
For in their shiny world hearts don't speak.
I told her to loosen the lock and break free,
For nothing matters more than her mental peace.
They hardly care and come around as they please.
I told her so time and again,
They play mind games and she is left trapped and broken,
Keep close to those genuine few,
Who hold her dear and true.
She sits again at the window sill,
And returns disappointed.

BLOCKED

It's a weekend morning,
I struggle to write.
They tell me you've not written anything for a while.
I stay silent like my paper sitting absolutely blank.
The words are not quite there,
I affirm unsure.
I go back in time and think about the future,
Struggling to stay in the present,
For I feel my growth now stunting.
My goals, a little too overworked, over-thought.
My mind, too preoccupied, too overwhelmed.
My heart too silent, too suppressed.
I keep my feelings closed,
Careful not to over-share.
For too many pretend to understand but none try to listen and register.
I flip my pen over as my thoughts feel too heavy and structure too loose,
I don't feel I can pen down a piece with such chaos.
My paper sits blank,
I struggle to write,
As my calendar now changes to Monday.

CLASPED

Clasped between my fingers,
Is the love you dearly placed.
Struggling to stay, eager to leave,
Careful not to hurt but nonetheless hurting.
Your hand grips tighter, my waist twists and then sits still,
Pretty just as you like.
I look up the ceiling not feeling all that pretty as you think I do,
My veins, they pop up as you send shivers all over my body.
My mind phases out,
Clarity seems far and lines blur as our palms grip tighter.
Just another day when my feelings feel unclear,
You kiss the lines now formed on my forehead and they ease up.
It feels okay,
But you walk away leaving the door ajar.
Leaving your love,
Clasped between my fingers.

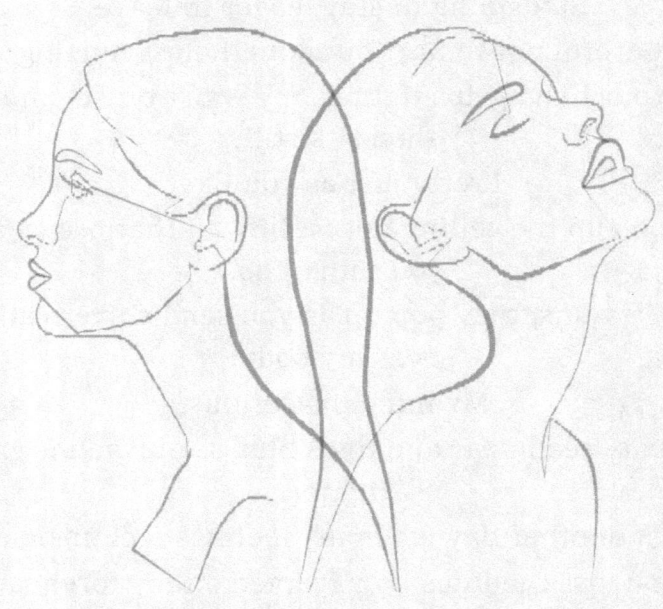

THE DEVIL

Banished into darkness with a few words and rays of ink,
Refusing change or submission.
Putting out my hand, only to retreat from painful touch.
My silence has a voice,
It's deafening.
I tear up the pages and break pointy instruments filled with blue,
Smear my face to conceal my truth.
I let them perceive the good,
Hiding away my darkness that never outgrows.
For a devil resides in me,
It screams, it plots, it thinks.
Tick tock tick tock.
Toxic.
They hold my hand but hardly feel the burning, the thumping, the maniac reactions inside of me.
They don't know me,
They don't know my feelings,
They don't understand.
My doors are thick, my walls towered up of unbreakable bricks,
I don't cower down from their tasteless whimpers.
My devil keeps me mad and sane at the same time,
Still waters run deep,
And rightly so.
I scratch, I bite, I break, I destroy.
Tick tock tick tock.
My devil thinks.
My devil conquers.

ALONG THE LINES

I trace my fingers along the lines in your palm,
Finding my comfort in their crookedness.
For I've waited long enough to feel something,
Some place where I can just be, 'Me'.
No filters.
No apologies.
No boundaries.
You gently tuck the hair strand at the back of my ear,
Though I purposely let it fall out again.
I've seen the scars you wear so bravely,
The tears you hide behind those dimples.
The troubles that make your heartbeats louder, faster.
I caress your hair in hopes of easing the pain you hide.
Those eyes, they speak volumes,
My eyes, they meet yours in the middle
so you can't look away.
So you stay.
Silent.
Calm.
Communicating.
I open your fingers from your fist,
So you let go of holding on too tight.
And time, it flies.
So I quickly get back to tracing my fingers
along the lines in your palm.

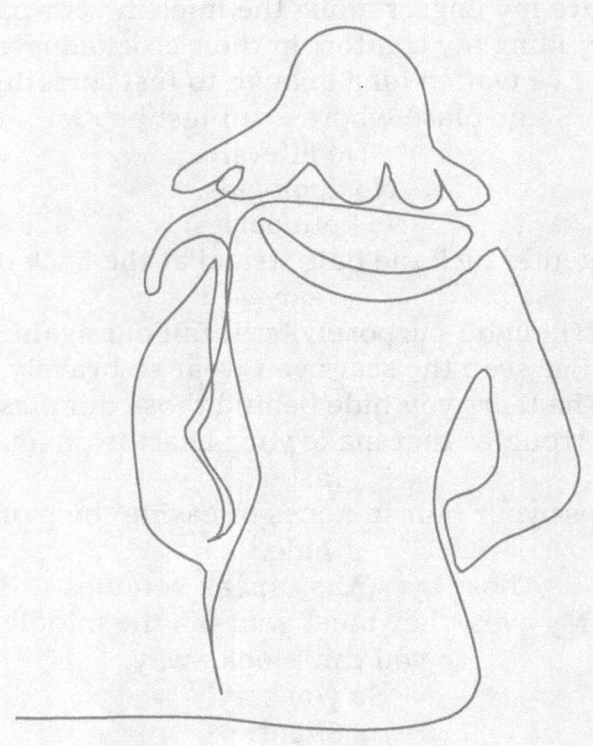

LETTING GO

Was it easy to let go?
It's been a while and I still hold on to his t-shirt.
Its scent has faded but I keep it close to
remember how it felt.
And it floods my mind,
The memories, all trapped in my closed eyes.
His laughter rings loud and clear,
I smile and then let out a tear.
Was it easy letting go?
Will it ever be?
They told me time heals.
Do they know that time also remembers?
It has a storage space that never erases.
My mind collaborates to keep the memories
fresh,
As if his touch was not distant, as if his hands
were holding on to mine.
For as I sit down to write,
My pen wreaks of his deep blue jeans,
My sheets of his slippery hair,
My pillows of his embrace.
We're in different worlds now.
Does his world ever think of me?
Does he look back like I do?
Or did he figure out the easiest way to let go.
I let the water trickle down my spine just like his
fingers would make their way slowly.
Can I turn the water off?
Will I let go?
Ever?

STICK FIGURES

Stick figures with cold hearts,
Run around with malice in their eyes,
daggers in their hands and hatred spewing from their mouth.
Selective listening and selective pleasing,
Their veins carry greed,
Selfish motives hidden behind those wide white teeth.
Stick figures with cold hearts,
They thrive on pain with fuming red burning from their face.
They settle on extremes,
With no middle ground,
A stranger to virtues.
Stick figures with cold hearts,
They feed on your soul, run you dry,
Till you feel empty inside.
Stick figures with cold hearts,
Roaming fulfilled, collecting glass shards.

NORMALISE BEING YOU

Normalise dusty, rusty, crooked, weird, not the usual.
For life has its ups and downs,
Walk the broken path,
And rise on a new leaf.
The sunshine has a harsh side too,
The moon shines with its imperfections.
Don't look away,
Look yourself in the eye.
You're here to rise up and fall.
You're here to continue.
You're here to be who you want to be.
Normalise having bad days,
Normalise imperfections,
Normalise real issues,
Break the life displayed on stands, social media and the like.
Normalise being you.

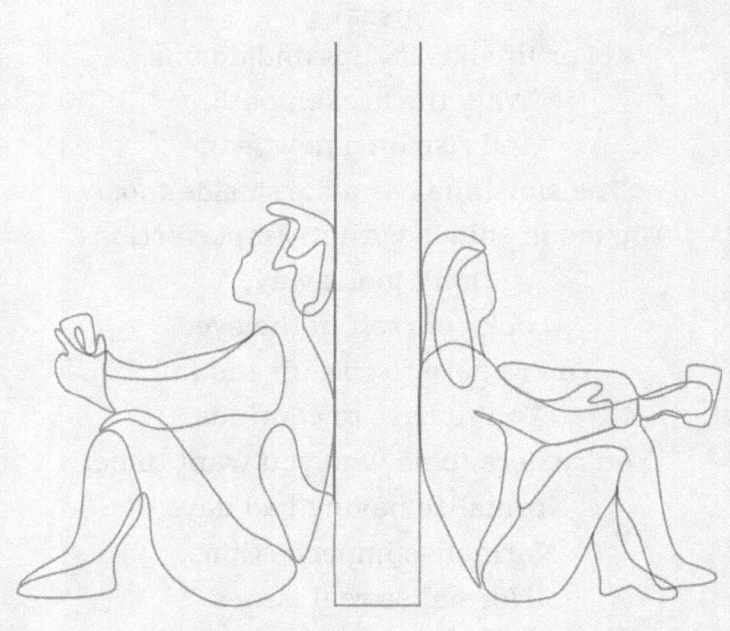

NOBODY

In seconds his demeanour changed,
Like I was nobody all of a sudden.
My truth was too harsh for him to understand,
And he had just scratched the surface.
For I hide my truth well underneath the layers,
I fear judgement,
Even though I claim I don't.
He's too unknown of life's hardships,
I live them everyday.
I've kept it inside.
My truth, it hurts, it bleeds, it burdens,
But I have to keep it safe.
For the judgement will always stay,
Even though he claims it won't.

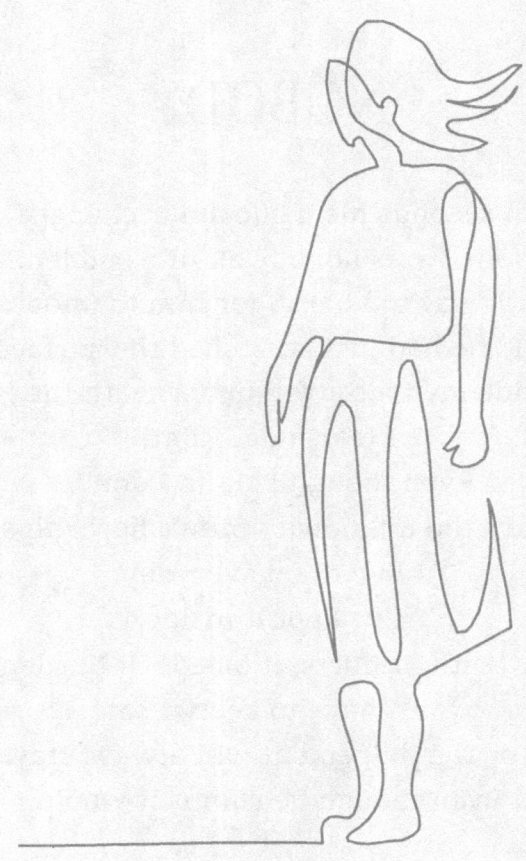

ESCAPE

I let my shutters down,
My skin
unshaven, pale and bare.
Unkempt hair with edges rough,
Letting loose a sudden outburst out of the ordinary.
Tired of looking out for endless hours,
A cage that's locked, now beginning to rust.
The tip of my nails crooked,
The flow in my veins in a silent rush.
Words ring in my ear,
But have no effect.
My eyes wander with a sense of longing,
A longing that stays undefined.
The whole of my parts,
And the parts of my whole,
Disintegrate at the slightest ray of escape.

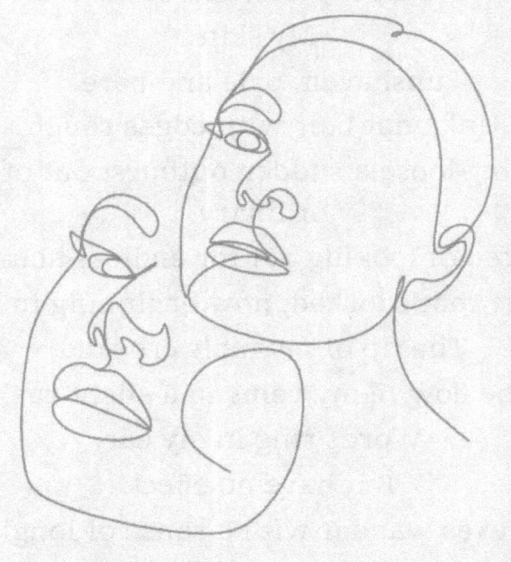

CIRCUS

The ringmaster keeps resigning and assuming
power at different intervals of time,
With performances in cut throat competition.
Tips and tricks flashing through, sifting
past one act after the other.
Puppets dancing on sold tunes,
Painting faces to hide their true-self,
Ruling over hired puppets with muted speech.
It is a game the world loves to watch and play,
Filling the space with deafening laughter and
applause

A LITTLE LESS HOPE

I trace my fingers along the lines in your palm,
Finding my comfort in their crookedness.
For I've waited long enough to feel something,
Some place where I can just be, 'Me'.
No filters.
No apologies.
No boundaries.
You gently tuck the hair strand at the back of my ear,
Though I purposely let it fall out again.
I've seen the scars you wear so bravely,
The tears you hide behind those dimples,
The troubles that make your heartbeats louder,
faster.
I caress your hair in hopes of easing the pain you hide.
Those eyes, they speak volumes
My eyes, they meet yours in the middle so you can't look away.
So you stay.
Silent.
Calm.
Communicating.
I open your fingers from your fist,
So you let go of holding too tight.
And time, it flies.
So I quickly get back to tracing my fingers along the lines in your palm.

DISMANTLING

The voices went silent,
As I opened my mouth to speak.
I had practiced from morning till night,
Picking myself up from diminishing courage.
Who knew?
Who tried to know?
They built a wall around their ears.
I spoke, my confidence not ready to dwindle by their
uninterested response.
I spoke.
I wanted to.
They stopped me, muted my speech.
And each time I tried getting up, dusting off, starting
with the same passion,
Something died inside.
They faked promises of fuelling my passion,
Instead cut my means.
The path I had created with blood and sweat felt lost, disregarded.
For in a world full of lies,
We make promises to uplift, but we fail.
We fail miserably in fulfilling them.
As we feast on dreams, flame their worth,
Reign mercilessly, unvalidated on a self-anointed throne.

We forget the feeling, the meaning of hope in those shiny eyes,
Which have created something from scratch.
We forget the struggle that the person underwent
just to stand in front of you.
You promised to create wildfires,
But you've created defeated soldiers.
No ounce of will let alone hope,
Their broken had forced fixes all this while.
But, their 'broken', refuses to, now.
You've turned them into empty vessels,
Empty vessels that don't make noise.

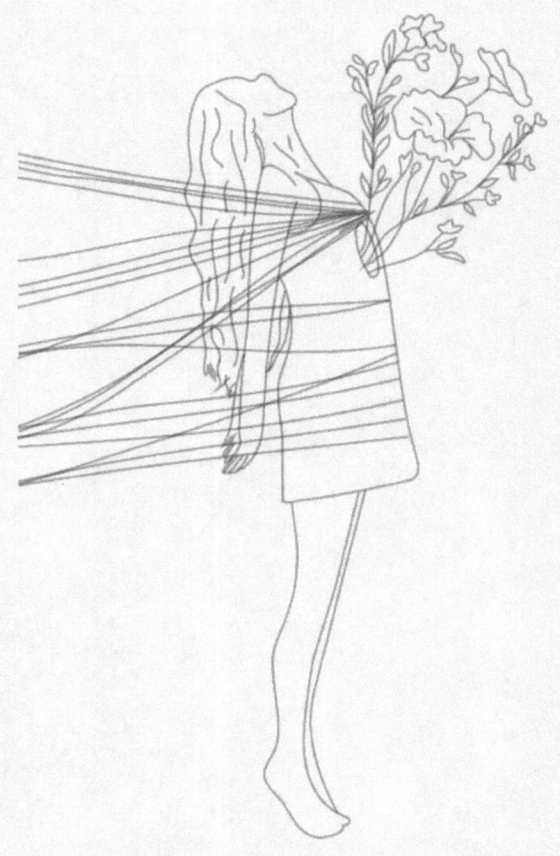

STRINGS OF MY LIFE

Growing up I was introduced to the strings of my life.
At first I felt nothing as they were subtle pulls.
Those strings of mine,
I wasn't sure,
Were they a part of me?
For as long as I can remember discovering it didn't always amount to it being in my hands,
As subtle pulls turned into broken strings, manipulated with knotted ties.
Those strings are mine, a part of me,
But yet not in my control.
My strings feel strong and speak their mind,
They formulate plans,
Living vicariously through the bubble that is freedom.
My strings have hidden dreams retreating from their tips,
My strings they say are mine,
As they hypocritically detach my rights.
They let my strings dream but not breathe,
They let my strings flow,
But only just as far.
My strings have endured screenings,
Filtered to the point I find hard to recognise.
My withered strings weathered with fleeting time.

My strings get tangled into a vicious circle where they go unheard, with ends split and taught to adjust.
My strings they evolve,
They slide through the strands of my hair, they fight as they flow from my mouth, my mouth which was tongue-tied.
The strings are mine, and mine to keep.
Falling deaf to the noise,
as they emerge fiercely through evolution from knotted ties.

THE POLE OF SERENDIPITY

These hands
gave way to lovers who held them tight for a while.
Fists closed on them
to stay strong and aloof.
Fingers cowering away on slightest of touches,
Too careful for,
Overflowing hearts and packed spaces.
With palms whole and lines broken,
Veins protruding and sinking.
Just this once
after fleeted time,
The hands went reckless, held on tight.
The touch of chance,
Awoke a feeling long forgotten.
The grip grew firm,
Midst overflowing hearts and packed spaces.

TUNES

He tells me tunes,
I don't want to hear.
His long conversations coupled with my fragments of attention.
He ushers me to check if I was listening,
I cluelessly nod, unsure of forming words.
Words which came easy to me,
Somehow get botched up and retreat from the tip of my tongue.
I look at him from my phone screen,
Not actually looking.
Hard to feel something,
When it's routine.
I sift through pages,
To drink up some words.
But this web of monotony is a stronger blow.
My words on text have become scarce,
And my face speaks more than my mouth.
Days on end I find I've lost track of who I was,
The arrogance of clarity pushed under the fresh pile of confusion.
He tells me tunes,
And it is just another day,
My lips are parched and my heart still pretends to skip a beat.

RUNNING IN YOUR THOUGHTS

What if I get a chance of running in your thoughts?
Would I be surprised, confused or lost?
Would all my curiosity finally come to a full stop?
When I'd come to know about the meaning behind your long blank gazes,
About the folding of your fingers,
or swallowed phrases.
What if I get a chance of running in your thoughts?
Would I be surprised, confused or lost?

THE TWO OF US

Back to the first night we met,
Where sparks flew.
A little high, a little low,
We were on the get-go.
You took me by the hand,
And we slow-danced on the floor.
I could feel every inch of you,
As your eyes looked into mine,
An ocean waiting to free-flow.
Cut to the present,
It's been a while now.
I wonder when to give in,
I wonder when to hold back,
You see I'm a little scared,
And you're not helping me much.
We've been hurt before,
So stay close, don't lose your touch.
These cracks in our communication,
Need to heal quickly.
Don't let them grow wider,
Anymore.
The 'Us' needs building,
It's not yet matured to crack.
I'm still searching the corners of you,
Reading each page, noting all clues.
Are you holding my hand tight?
Or do you plan to let go.
I'm starting to fall for you,
So don't let go.
Stay close, stay close.

KARMA

The days gone by are now forgotten poems to me.
Like everything you touched is now crumbled and meek.
I wish I could feel something more,
But there is nothing more left to feel.
I once wrote you a poem,
But it stands buried in the thickness of 100 sheets.
Scaring has not been your forte,
Scarring definitely.
How does it feel to be you?
A self-proclaimed godman,
Who stays ignorant of his dues.
In this life everyone has to pay,
It's better you pray than find your next prey.
The days gone by are now forgotten poems to me,
What you sow is what you'll see.

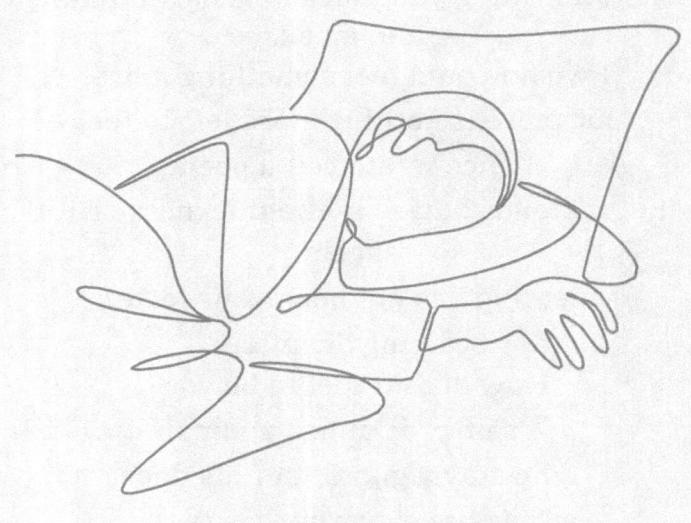

REWIND

I hoped for a happily ever after,
But an evil eye ruined it all.
When it all felt right,
A thunderstorm destructed everything.
A piercing pain strikes hard in my chest,
An unpleasant tingle in my heart.
I hoped for it to work out,
But the evil eye dwindled with the only good thing.
My life feels lifeless,
My journey a rocky path,
Many preyed on me,
Many I let prey,
For what?
I ask myself now.
But I don't have an answer,
I don't have the power,
I don't feel any more.
Am I walking dead now?
Am I a frozen bird amidst windy normalcy?
I don't know what's next.
It feels blue,
Whenever I see you.
Your face all broken,
Your eyes staring hurt,
I wish I could rewind and restart.
I wish I could not hurt you like I did.
I wished so much,
Yet I failed.
Hope I can rise again,
And make it all happen for us.

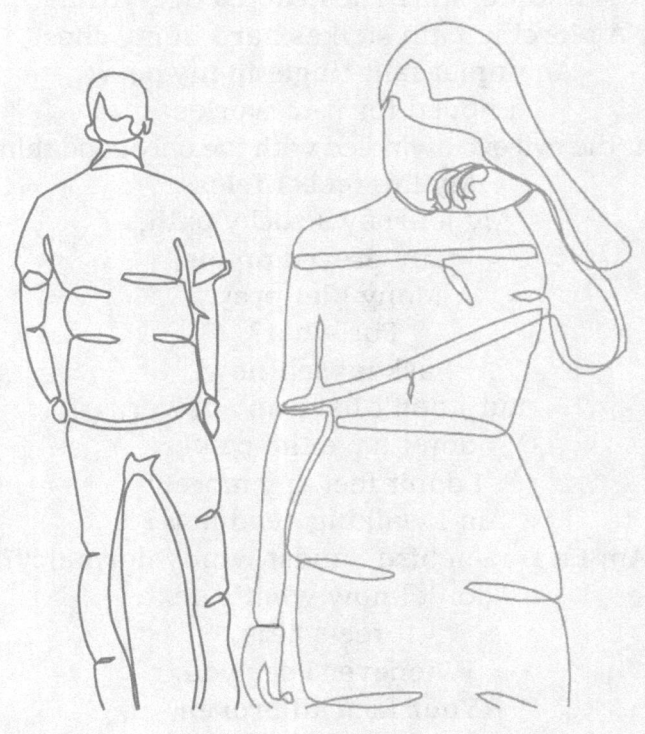

BROKEN BONDS

The silent screams that no one hears.
Subdued cries all deaf on ears.
Unsaid understanding, a hyperbole.
A little faith too much to hold,
A naughty element, an easy invader.
Years of friendship fallen flat,
For-granted, for-granted forgiven.
A hammered heart gets worn out,
A lonely soul grows lonelier,
A disappointed face gets sadder,
A broken bone gets shattered,
The silent screams that no one hears,
Subdued cries all deaf on ears.

STROKES OF FATE

Strokes of fate brought us together,
A little messed up,
We navigated through our chaos.
We're in it for the wrongs turns,
We're in it for the long run,
We're in when we feel done,
We're in it for the fun,
We're in it to become one.
So next time you come knocking at my door,
Hope you seal it with 'forever'.

DESOLATE

Innocence carefully wrapped around sinister intent,
The souls rot in slow-moving life.
Smiles wide at sunrise,
Evil grin by the night.
No one knows what goes around,
Slaves of the devil run covered in broad daylight.
The right from wrong and wrong from right,
It is all mixed up.
Innocence carefully wrapped around sinister intent,
The souls rot in slow-moving life.

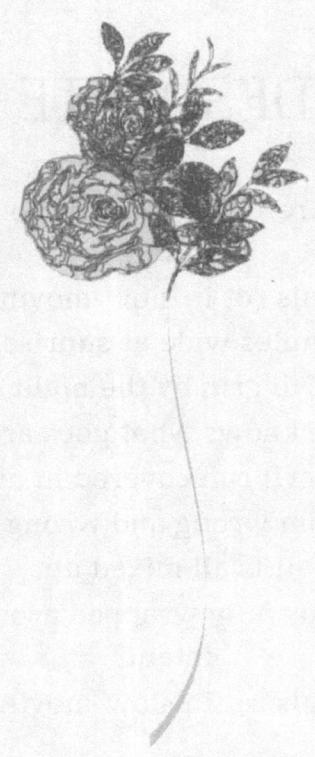

Life is real! Life is earnest!
And the grave is not its goal;
Dust thou art, to dust returnest,
Was not spoken of the soul.
- Henry Wadsworth Longfellow

ABOUT THE AUTHOR

raghavi.jhanjee99@gmail.com

the_regularteenager

Raghavi Jhanjee is a poetic soul and a copywriter in the vibrant world of advertising.

Her verses breathe life into emotions, weaving a tapestry of thoughts that resonate with the human experience.

With a heart that beats to the rhythm of poetry, Raghavi passionately shares her introspections and musings through the art of words.

Beyond the realms of advertising, she finds solace in the enchanting worlds of travel, literature, and dance.

Metaphors flow effortlessly from her, adding depth and nuance to her poetic expressions.

Follow her Instagram poetry blog, where she invites you to join her on a journey of emotions and reflections.

Connect with her poetic world @the_regularteenager, where every verse is a window
into her imagination.

ABOUT THE ILLUSTRATOR

anghosh28.ag@gmail.com

miss_anusreeghosh

Hello there, I'm Anusree Ghosh, a passionate illustrator and graphic designer entrenched in the dynamic realm of the advertising industry. My canvas is not just confined to pixels and vectors; it's an exciting playground where ideas come to life.

With a flair for injecting humor and a fun-loving personality, my work mirrors my vibrant spirit. Each design is a testament to my commitment to turning mundane concepts into visually captivating masterpieces.

In the world of advertising, where every detail counts, I thrive on infusing a sense of playfulness into my creations.

ABOUT THE ART DIRECTOR

✉ *abhirup.rocks2011@gmail.com*

◉ *idripwaytoohard*

Meet Abhirup Chowdhury, the Art Director extraordinaire in the advertising realm.
Passion fuels my role as I orchestrate captivating visual narratives, seamlessly blending strategic prowess with artistic innovation.
Each project is a canvas for creativity, where he leads teams in crafting compelling campaigns that leave a lasting impact.
With an eye on industry trends and a heart dedicated to the art of communication, he's on a mission to redefine visual storytelling in the dynamic world of advertising

EMBRACE

Embrace encapsulates the author's experiences while she was growing up. Incited by her profound
feelings and ruminations about various situations and relationships, she pens down her poems that reflect her organic emotions and her in-depth perspective about life.

YOUR EXPERIENCE

www.ingramcontent.com/pod-product-compliance
Lightning Source LLC
LaVergne TN
LVHW041606070526
838199LV00052B/3013